Disney

Adventurers
™

STORY COLLECTION

Disney
PRESS

NEW YORK

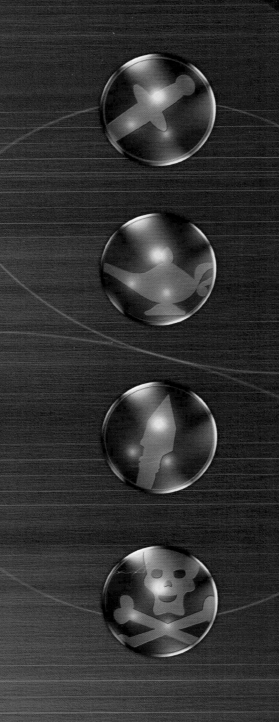

Disney's HERCULES

5

Disney's Aladdin

101

Disney's TARZAN

197

Walt Disney's Peter Pan

261

Disney's HERCULES

Pay attention! Yes, we're talkin' to you.
Perhaps you've seen us on a vase or two?
We're the Muses, and you won't believe
The fantastic story that's up our sleeve.

Long ago, when the world was just made,
Some horrible Titans made the people afraid.
Volcanoes erupted, there were storms and earthquakes—
The earth was a mess, but, hey! Those are the breaks!

Then the boss-man, Zeus, threw those guys in a hole.
To make order from chaos was his ultimate goal.
He assigned each god and goddess a job to do,
And the people were grateful—their troubles were few!
But one day something happened way up on high
That would change history in the blink of an eye…

Fireworks lit up the sky over Mount Olympus, home of the gods, to celebrate the arrival of Zeus and Hera's son, Hercules. It was obvious to everyone that this was no ordinary baby. He was cute and cuddly, to be sure, but also unbelievably strong. Why, he could easily lift his mighty father above his head!

All the Olympian gods attended the celebration, bringing an array of amazing presents. But Zeus was not to be outdone. He spun several clouds into an adorable winged baby horse as a present to Baby Hercules from himself and Hera. "His name is Pegasus, and he's all yours, Son," Zeus said, beaming.

Soon, Hades, the god of the Underworld, appeared. He hated Zeus for putting him in charge of a place that was full of dead people. But Zeus was Hades' boss, after all, so Hades just smiled sweetly and handed Baby Hercules a pacifier—shaped like a skeleton.

Baby Hercules grabbed Hades' hand and squeezed it until Hades reeled in pain. "He's going to be the strongest of all the gods," Zeus announced proudly.

Hades quickly left the party on Olympus and headed back to the Underworld, his temper—and his hair—flaring. He was making plans for the day when he would overthrow Zeus and rule the universe.

When he docked at the Underworld, his two henchmen, Pain and Panic, told him that the Fates had arrived.

The Fates were three hideous old women who could see the past, present, and future with the one eye they shared. They were in charge of cutting a person's Thread of Life, sending each one straight to the Underworld.

"So, is this Hercules kid gonna mess up my plan to take over Olympus, or what?" an anxious Hades asked them. They refused to say, so Hades resorted to flattery. "Did you get your hair cut? Get a makeover? You look fabulous!" he told the shriveled old crones.

The Fates relented, telling Hades that in eighteen years, when the planets became perfectly aligned, Hades could indeed overthrow Zeus. "But," they added, "if Hercules fights on the side of the gods, you will fail."

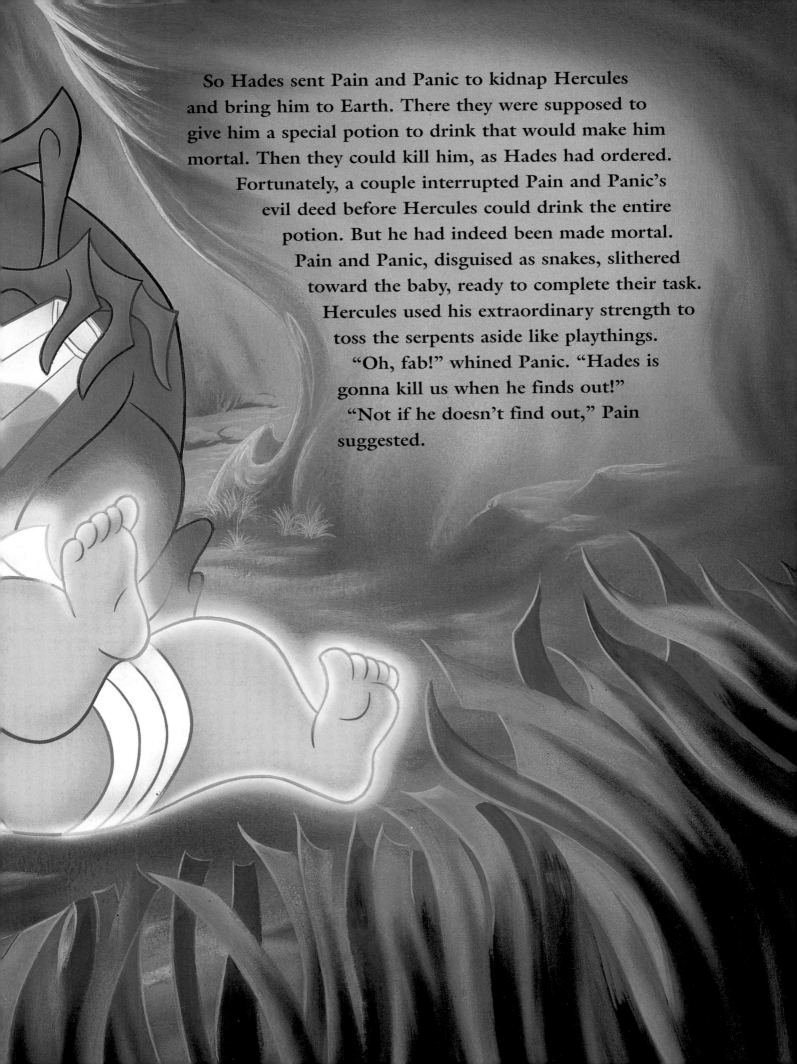

So Hades sent Pain and Panic to kidnap Hercules
and bring him to Earth. There they were supposed to
give him a special potion to drink that would make him
mortal. Then they could kill him, as Hades had ordered.
Fortunately, a couple interrupted Pain and Panic's
evil deed before Hercules could drink the entire
potion. But he had indeed been made mortal.
Pain and Panic, disguised as snakes, slithered
toward the baby, ready to complete their task.
Hercules used his extraordinary strength to
toss the serpents aside like playthings.
"Oh, fab!" whined Panic. "Hades is
gonna kill us when he finds out!"
"Not if he doesn't find out," Pain
suggested.

20

Now that Hercules was mortal, he could not return
to Olympus. Zeus and Hera could only watch sadly from
above as their baby was adopted by the childless couple,
Amphitryon and Alcmene.

Under his adopted parents' loving care, Hercules grew into a devoted
son. He tried to use his great strength to help out—like the time he
replaced their donkey, Penelope, when she became lame on the way to the
marketplace. Unfortunately, he usually wasn't able to control his strength.
People avoided Hercules because, wherever he went, disaster often followed.

For example, one day in the marketplace, Hercules wanted to join some of the boys in a game of discus.

"Sorry, Herc. We've already got five, and we want to keep it an even number," they said, clumsily turning him down.

Nevertheless, the eager Hercules ran after their discus, knocking into the pillars of the marketplace and leaving it in ruins. The townspeople had enough, and warned his father to keep him away.

"I'll never fit in around here!" Hercules lamented.

Hercules knew there had to be someplace where he would fit in—where he wouldn't feel like an outsider.

He told his parents he had to find out where he belonged. They decided the time was right to show him the gold medallion he had been wearing when they found him.

"It has the symbol of the gods on it," Alcmene explained.

"Maybe they have the answers I'm looking for," Hercules mused.

Now he knew he should begin his quest at the temple of Zeus.

With heavy hearts, Hercules and his parents bid each other good-bye.

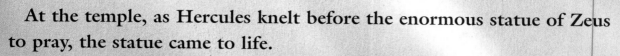

At the temple, as Hercules knelt before the enormous statue of Zeus to pray, the statue came to life.

"EEEEOWW!" screamed Hercules, running away from the giant figure.

"Hey, hold on, kiddo! Is that the kind of hello you give your father?" Zeus asked him.

Hercules was confused! If Zeus was his father, then Hercules must be a god.

But Zeus explained that Hercules wasn't a god, he was human now—and humans were not allowed on Olympus.

"You mean you can't do a thing?" Hercules asked in despair.

"I can't, but you can," Zeus explained. "You must prove yourself a true hero on Earth," Zeus told him. "Begin by seeking out Philoctetes, the trainer of heroes, on the Isle of Idra." Then, to help him on his way, Zeus reunited Hercules with his old pal Pegasus.

"I won't let you down, Father!" called Hercules as he and Pegasus flew off toward Idra.

Hercules was surprised to discover that Philoctetes was a wisecracking little satyr—a half-man, half-goat creature, complete with horns. Hercules told Phil about his dream of being a hero and asked the trainer to help him.

"I had a dream once, too—that I was gonna train the greatest hero there ever was!" Phil declared. "So great, the gods would hang a picture of him in the stars." Then Phil explained that everyone he had ever tried to help had disappointed him—especially Achilles. "Now there was a guy who had it all! The build, the foot speed...he could keep on coming. But that furshlugginer heel of his! Dreams are for rookies," he continued. "A guy can only take so much disappointment."

Hercules tried to convince Phil that he was special by demonstrating his remarkable strength. "I'm different from those other guys!" Hercules insisted. "I can go the distance!" He even revealed to Phil that he was the son of Zeus.

"Zeus? The big guy?" asked Phil in disbelief. "Mr. Lightning Bolts?"

Hercules swore it was the truth, yet Phil still refused—until Zeus sent a lightning bolt his way.

"Okay!" Phil agreed, convinced. "You win!"

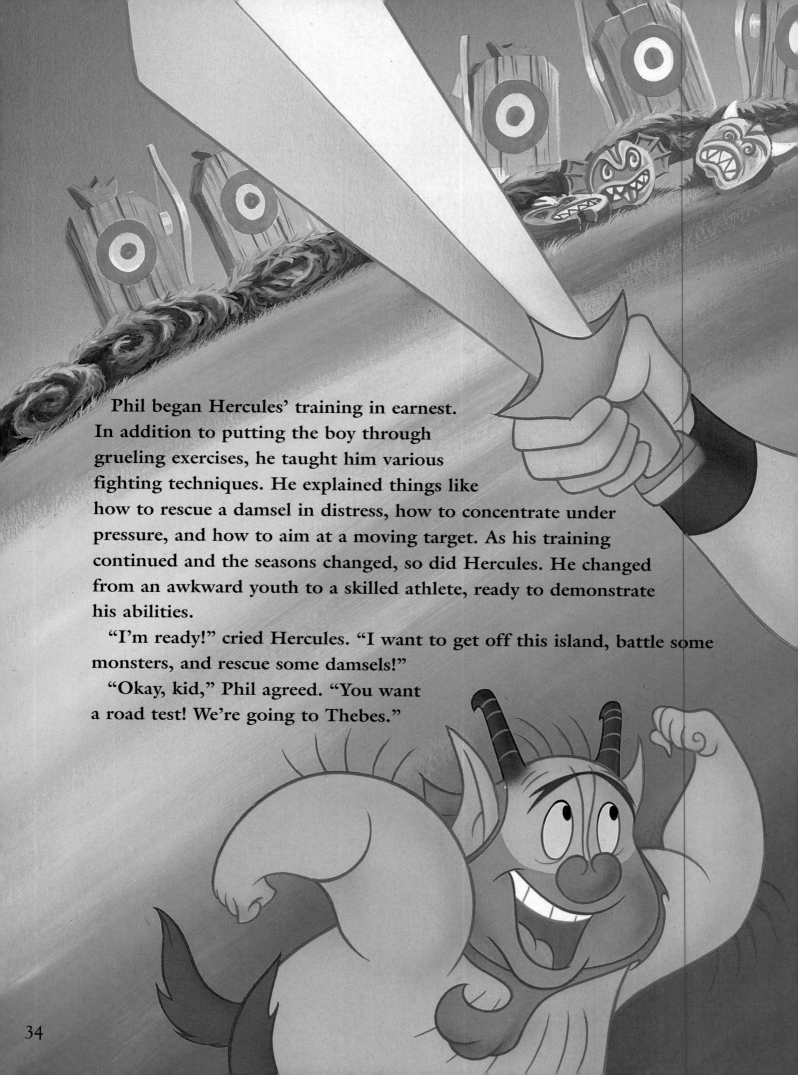

Phil began Hercules' training in earnest.
In addition to putting the boy through
grueling exercises, he taught him various
fighting techniques. He explained things like
how to rescue a damsel in distress, how to concentrate under
pressure, and how to aim at a moving target. As his training
continued and the seasons changed, so did Hercules. He changed
from an awkward youth to a skilled athlete, ready to demonstrate
his abilities.

"I'm ready!" cried Hercules. "I want to get off this island, battle some
monsters, and rescue some damsels!"

"Okay, kid," Phil agreed. "You want
a road test! We're going to Thebes."

On the way to Thebes, they came upon Meg, a beautiful and self-assured young woman who was in the clutches of a burly centaur named Nessus.

"Back off, Atlas," Meg snapped at Hercules when he tried to help. But Hercules—eager to rack up hero points—fought with the centaur anyway.

Hercules won, even though Phil wasn't too crazy about his fighting technique.

With Nessus out of the picture, Hercules tried to introduce himself to Meg, but he became shy and tongue-tied.

Phil didn't like all the attention Hercules was paying to her. After all, a hero shouldn't have any distractions. Pegasus wasn't crazy about this gal, either. In fact, he was downright jealous! When Hercules offered Meg a ride, the horse flew up into a tree.

"I'll be all right," Meg assured Hercules as she walked off. "I can tie my own sandals and everything. Bye-bye, Wonder Boy."

But now Meg was in trouble. She had to explain to her boss, Hades, that some strongman named Hercules had chased the centaur off and she wasn't able to recruit him.

Hades became inflamed when he heard that Hercules was alive! "Dead as a doornail," he spat at Pain and Panic. "Weren't those your exact words?" Hades grabbed his henchmen by their long, slithery tails.

"At least we made him mortal," they stammered.

So Hades hatched a plot to get rid of Hercules once and for all.

Meanwhile, in Thebes, Hercules announced that he was the hero for them. The Thebans just rolled their eyes. No hero had ever been able to stop the fires, earthquakes, and floods that had plagued them.

"You'll get your chance," Phil told him. "All we need is a catastrophe."

Right on cue, Meg appeared. "Two little boys are trapped by a rock slide!" she cried. Hercules was thrilled. This was his chance!

As the townsfolk crowded around the edge of the canyon, Hercules lifted a massive boulder high over his head, freeing the boys. Hercules waited, but only a few people applauded. The Thebans were a tough audience! The boys scampered up the canyon. They stopped at Hades' feet and changed back into Pain and Panic.

Moments later, Phil joined Hercules in the canyon, and the two became aware of a weird hissing sound.

Suddenly there was a crack of lightning, and a gigantic dragonlike creature—the Hydra—emerged from the mouth of a cave. Phil ran for cover while Hercules, sword drawn, battled the beast until it threw him into the air and swallowed him whole.

But after a moment, Hercules slashed his way out of the monster's throat and sent its head toppling to the ground.

Pain and Panic stole nervous glances at Hades, but the hotheaded god was strangely relaxed. For the Hydra was not dead. Three writhing heads emerged from a wound in her neck. Hercules, atop Pegasus, sliced at them with his sword, but each time he did, they multiplied!

"Forget the head-slicing thing!" Phil coached. "It's not working!"

Finally the enormous creature pinned Hercules to a cliff with a claw. Thinking quickly, Hercules smashed his fist into the mountain, causing an avalanche that buried him and the Hydra under a mountain of rocks. But then Hercules shocked everyone by emerging from the Hydra's claw unharmed!

Hold the phone, we just gotta break in!
This is where Herc's fame and fortune begin.
From that day on he had battles galore...
Boars, harpies, sea monsters, lions, and more!
He had gone from a nothing, a no one, a zero,
To a champion, a star, a celebrity hero!
Fans and groupies cheered wherever he went.
Did we mention his handprints got put in cement?

Even Pain and Panic couldn't resist the Hercules-mania sweeping the land. During a "get Hercules" strategy session, Hades noticed that Pain was wearing a new pair of Hercules sandals, and Panic was slurping on a cup of "Herculade" sports drink.

Hades started burning up. "I've got twenty-four hours to get rid of this bozo or the entire scheme I've been setting up for eighteen years goes up in smoke...AND YOU'RE WEARING HIS MERCHANDISE!" he shrieked.

Hades cooled down. "He's got to have a weakness,"
he said. "For Pandora, it was the box thing. The Trojans
bet on the wrong horse..."

Hades knew Meg could get close enough to Hercules to discover
his weakness. Then Hades could use it to destroy him. Meg refused,
but she had once made a deal with Hades, trading her freedom to save
her ex-boyfriend's life. Now she had to do what Hades wanted.
To sweeten the deal, Hades promised to release her if she succeeded.

Meanwhile, Hercules visited Zeus at the temple, reenacting some of his victories for his adoring father. But Zeus gently broke the news that Hercules was still not ready to rejoin the other gods on Mount Olympus.

"I'm the most famous person in all of Greece!" Hercules protested. "I mean, I'm an action figure!"

"My boy, I'm afraid that being famous isn't the same as being a true hero," Zeus explained. "Look inside your heart to discover what you must do."

Later, back at Hercules' villa, Phil ran down the list of the day's activities while Hercules posed for a vase painting. "...at noon ya got a luncheon with the Daughters of the Greek Revolution...at one ya got a meeting with King Augeus..."

But Hercules seemed distracted. "This isn't getting me anywhere," he sighed to Phil. "I'll never make it to Olympus."

They were interrupted when a group of Hercules' admirers burst into the room. Hercules hid while Phil herded the fans out, but one girl stayed behind. Hercules was thrilled to discover it was Meg.

"So," Meg wondered, "you look like you could use a break. Think your nanny goat would go berserk if you played hooky this afternoon?"

Hercules gladly ignored his duties as a celebrity, and the two went off to spend the day together. Meg questioned Hercules to discover his weaknesses, but realized he had none. Though she would not admit it to herself, Meg found herself falling in love.

When Phil caught up with them that evening he was hopping mad! Hercules reluctantly left for home, though he was so starry-eyed that he didn't even notice when Phil fell off Pegasus.

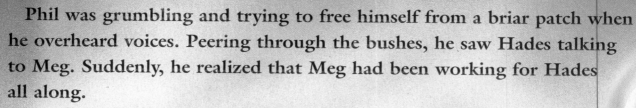

Phil was grumbling and trying to free himself from a briar patch when he overheard voices. Peering through the bushes, he saw Hades talking to Meg. Suddenly, he realized that Meg had been working for Hades all along.

"I knew that dame was trouble. This is gonna break the kid's heart," Phil said to himself as he raced off to tell Hercules the truth.

What was even worse was that Hades had discovered that Hercules did have a weakness—and that weakness was Meg.

When Phil found Hercules at the stadium, the young hero couldn't stop talking about how wonderful Meg was.

"Isn't she the brightest, funniest, most amazing girl you ever met?" Hercules gushed.

"Sure, but she's also a fraud," Phil insisted. "The whole thing is some kinda set-up!"

When Hercules became furious and refused to believe him, Phil told Hercules he was on his own. "I thought you were gonna be the all-time champ...not the all-time chump!" the trainer fumed. Saddened by Hercules' stubbornness, Phil left him alone to brood.

While Phil and Hercules were arguing, Pain and Panic went to work. The two transformed themselves into a beautiful female horse and pranced in front of Pegasus. Always a sucker for a pretty mane, Pegasus followed the filly into a nearby stable. But talk about a bad date—within seconds, his mare dissolved and changed back into Pain and Panic. Hades' henchmen tied Pegasus up and left him inside, unable to help Hercules should he need him.

Hercules would need him, and soon. As the alignment of the planets approached, Hades was becoming desperate. He went to the stadium to plead his case to Hercules. He tried to play it cool—which was very hard for such a hotheaded guy to do.

"I would be eternally grateful if you would just take one day off from this hero business of yours," Hades said casually. "I mean, monsters, natural disasters...they can wait a day, okay?"

Suspecting that people would get hurt, Hercules refused—until Hades revealed Meg, bound at his side.

Now Hercules was forced to make a deal. If Hercules would give up his strength for one day, Hades promised that Meg would be safe. Hercules agreed. Then, when his strength was gone, Hades revealed that Meg had been working for him all along. Hercules faced the awful truth, weak and heartbroken.

When at last the planets aligned, Hades could free the Titans from their underground prison. "Brothers!" Hades bellowed. "Who locked you away in this prison? And if I let you out, what's the first thing you're gonna do?"

"Destroy him! Destroy Zeus!" thundered the Rock Titan, the Lava Titan, the Ice Titan, the Tornado Titan, and the one-eyed Cyclops as they emerged from the pit.

"Good answer!" Hades replied gleefully. Then he sent the Cyclops on a special mission to Thebes to hunt down Hercules and destroy him.

Hermes was napping peacefully on a cloud when a loud rumbling shook him awake. His eyes flew open to see the angry Titans approaching Mount Olympus.

"Uh-oh!" he said to himself. "We're in big trouble!"

He raced to tell Zeus, who ordered him to summon the gods for an immediate counterattack. Hephaestus hammered lightning bolts as weapons, and the other gods prepared themselves for battle. But the gods were no match for the Tornado Titan, who sucked them up like a vacuum cleaner.

In the meantime, down on Earth, Thebes was in flames. The people cried out for Hercules to save them as the Cyclops went on a rampage, leaving destruction in his path.

Though he no longer possessed his strength, Hercules confronted the Cyclops, who kicked him across the street like a pebble. Meg pleaded with Hercules not to fight the giant, but Hercules no longer cared what happened to him. Then Meg heard a familiar whinnying coming from a nearby stable. She discovered Pegasus and untied him, and the two set off in search of Phil. Meg believed that only Phil could get through to Hercules.

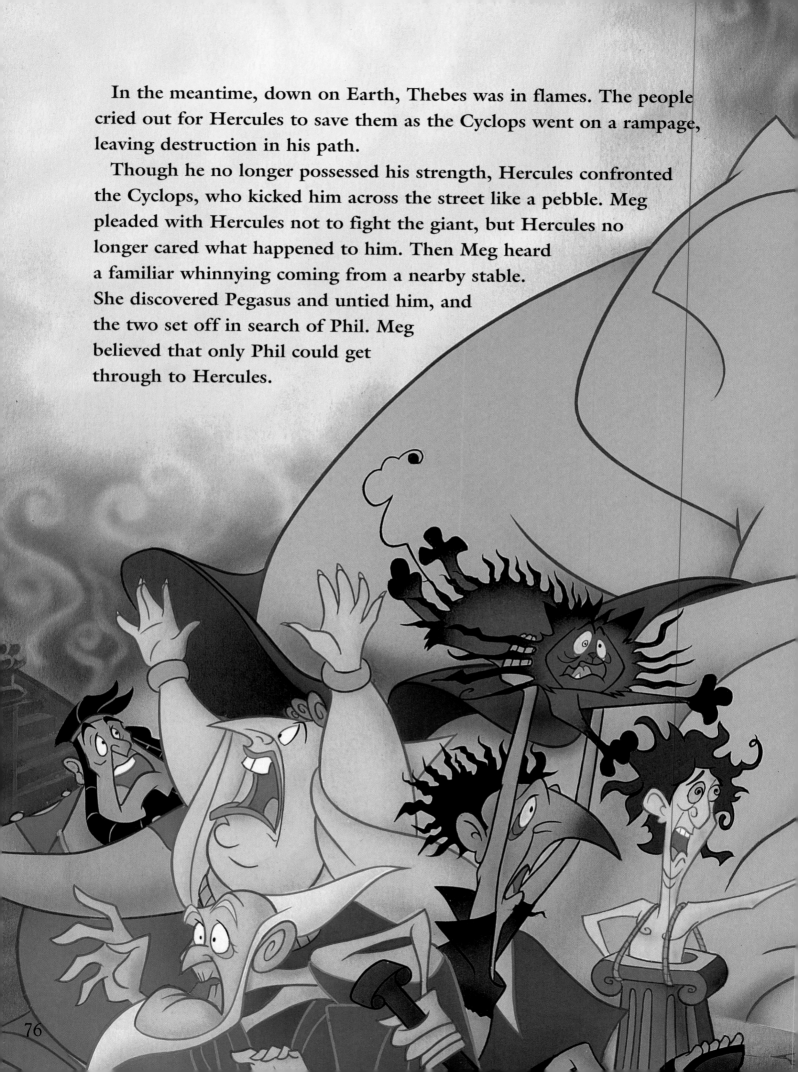

When they found him, Phil was about to board a boat leaving Thebes. "Hercules gave us something we'd both lost—hope!" Meg reminded him. "Now he's lost his hope! If you don't help him now, he'll die!" Hearing these words, Phil agreed to return to the city with her.

Up on Mount Olympus, Zeus was in trouble. All of the gods had been captured, and now he was out of lightning bolts.

"Hades!" exclaimed Zeus when the god of the Underworld appeared. "I should have known you were behind this!"

Then the Lava Titan arrived and surrounded Zeus with molten rock. To finish the job, the Ice Titan cooled the lava with his frigid breath. Zeus was soon encased in solid rock, unable to move.

Hercules was faring no better. When Phil and Meg found him, it was clear the Cyclops would finish him off in no time.

"C'mon, kid, fight back!" Phil pleaded. He encouraged Hercules not to lose sight of his dreams—or his belief in himself.

Hearing his words, Hercules' resolve returned. He grabbed a burning stick and thrust it at the monster's eye. The monster screamed and dropped Hercules.

82

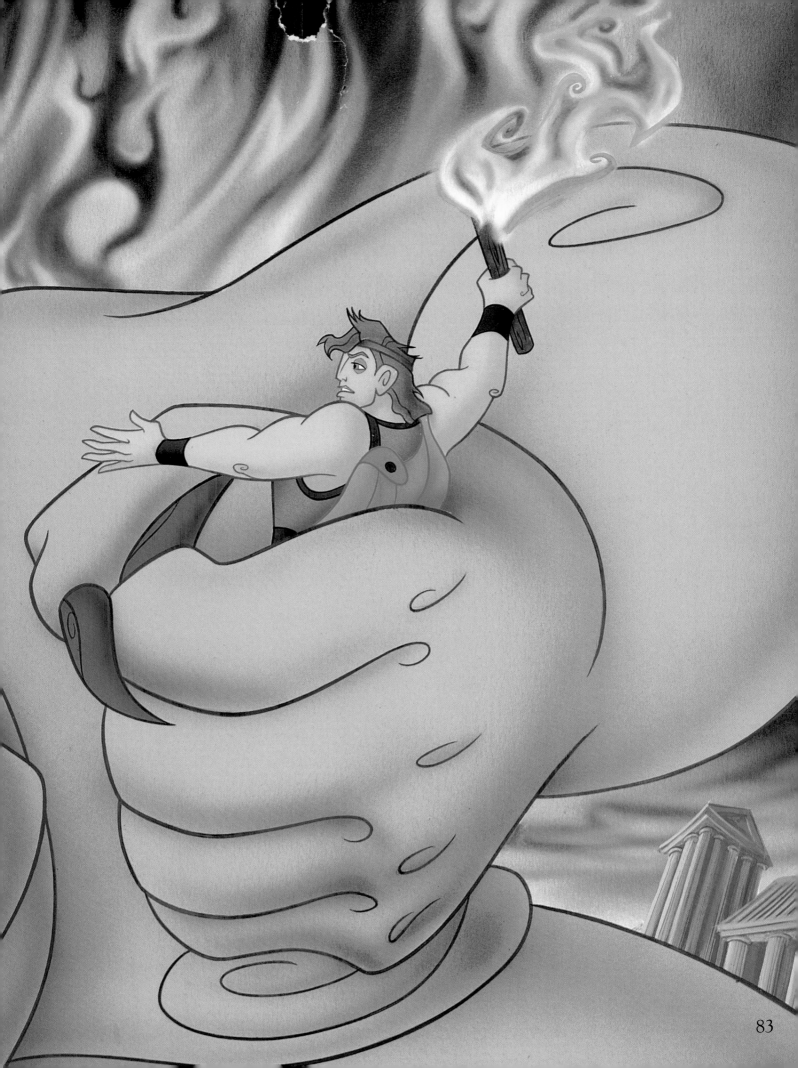

The Cyclops staggered over a cliff. Just then, a column the Cyclops had hit fell toward Hercules. Meg pushed him out of the way, so she was pinned instead. As Hercules tried to lift the pillar, his strength returned. "Hades' deal is broken," Meg explained weakly. "He promised I wouldn't get hurt. You must go to Olympus and stop him." Before he left her side, Meg finally admitted to Hercules that she loved him.

Hercules swept up to Mount Olympus, breaking the chains that bound the gods. Then, with his bare hands, he broke apart the lava that imprisoned his father, Zeus. Hephaestus rushed to fashion a new supply of lightning bolts, and the gods went back on the attack. Zeus and Hercules joined forces. Zeus's lightning bolts held the Titans back while Hercules used the Tornado Titan to swoop them up. Then Hercules hurled the Titans into space.

Knowing his plan was ruined, Hades started to make his getaway. "Thanks a ton, Wonder Boy," Hades began. "But I got one swell consolation prize. A friend of yours who's dying to see me."

Horrified, Hercules realized that Hades meant Meg.

Hercules raced back to her side, but it was too late. The Fates had cut Meg's Thread of Life.

"This wasn't supposed to happen!" Hercules cried in anguish.

"I'm sorry, kid," Phil said sadly. "But there are some things you can't change."

A look of determination came over Hercules' face. "Yes, I can," he replied as he mounted Pegasus once more.

When Hercules arrived in the Underworld, Hades already had Meg's spirit in the Pit of Death.

"You like making deals," Hercules said. "Take me in Meg's place."

This was an unexpected bonus, Hades thought. "Okay!" he agreed. "You get her out...she goes—you stay!"

Hercules dived into the Pit of Death to retrieve Meg's spirit, growing older and older until it was clear he was near death himself. But when the Fates tried to cut his Thread of Life, they were shocked to find that they could not.

Hercules carried Meg's spirit out of the pit.

"You can't be alive!" cried Hades. "You'd have to be a...a..."

"A god?" Pain and Panic offered helpfully.

Hades tried to smooth things over. "You and Zeus can take a little joke, right?" he asked. Hercules ignored him. Then Hades reached out to Meg's spirit and pleaded, "Meg! Meg, talk to him!"

That was enough! With a mighty fist, Hercules hurled Hades down into the Pit of Death. The spinning spirits of the dead dragged the lord of the Underworld down into their ghostly midst.

Hercules carried Meg's spirit back to her body. As soul and flesh reunited, her eyes fluttered open. She was alive! While Hercules and Meg held each other tight, Zeus lifted them to Mount Olympus on a cloud.

"A true hero isn't measured by the size of his strength, but by the strength of his heart," Zeus proclaimed. "Welcome home, Son!"

"Father, this is the moment I've always dreamed of," Hercules began. "But a life without Meg—even an immortal one—would be empty. I wish to stay on Earth with her. I finally know where I belong."

Zeus looked at Hera, who nodded her approval.

They would miss him, but Zeus and Hera knew that Hercules had found happiness at last. Their beloved son returned to a hero's welcome on Earth. In the cheering crowd were Herc's earthly parents, Alcmene and Amphitryon. Then someone pointed up to the sky, and everyone gazed in wonder at the constellation Zeus had created in his son's honor.

That is how the story ends—full of love and mirth.
Hercules was now a star in the heavens and on Earth.
And his friend Philoctetes at last had found a youth
Whose picture the gods put up in lights—and that's the gospel truth!

Disney's Aladdin

Welcome to Agrabah, city of enchantment, of mystery, of delight...where things are never as they seem. This lamp, for instance. It is no ordinary lamp. It once changed a young man's life. This young man, like this lamp, was more than he appeared. Come closer, and I will tell you his tale...

It all began one night out in the vast Arabian desert, where a dark man with a dark purpose sat waiting in the moonlight. His name was Jafar, and he was Grand Vizier to the Sultan of Agrabah.

Suddenly, from the shadows, a second man appeared. "You have it, Gazeem?" growled Jafar.

Gazeem held up one half of a golden scarab. "I had to slit a few throats, but I got it." Jafar lunged for the scarab, but Gazeem pulled it away. "First, where is the treasure you promised?" he asked.

"Trust me, my pungent friend," hissed Jafar as his parrot, Iago, ripped the scarab from Gazeem's hand. "You'll get what's coming to you."

Then, pulling the other half of the scarab out from his cloak, Jafar touched the two pieces together.

The scarab began to glow. Then it exploded into flight, leaving a gleaming path in its wake.

"Quickly!" yelled Jafar. "Follow the trail!"

The horsemen followed the magic scarab into the desert. At last it stopped its flight and buried itself in a mound of sand. And there, in the desert sand, a huge tiger head reared up.

"The Cave of Wonders!" exclaimed Jafar.

Jafar ordered Gazeem into the cave. "The treasure you find is yours, but the lamp is mine! Bring me the lamp!"

But as Gazeem stepped into the tiger's mouth, it roared. "Know this: Only one may enter here—one whose worth lies far within—a diamond in the rough!" Then the Cave of Wonders sank back into the sand, swallowing up the unworthy Gazeem.

"I must find this diamond in the rough," said Jafar.

Early the next morning, in the marketplace of Agrabah, a young man took a loaf of bread.

"Stop, you street rat!" shouted the Sultan's guards.

But there was no stopping Aladdin (for that was his name). He and his sidekick, Abu, fled over rooftops, onto balconies, through open doorways, up steps, and down alleyways, always one step ahead of the guards.

Outwitted, the guards gave up. Aladdin and Abu sat down to eat. But when Aladdin saw others even hungrier than he, he couldn't help himself. He had to give them the bread.

So Aladdin and Abu returned to their humble quarters...tired, hungry, and poor as ever.

Gazing at the Sultan's palace, Aladdin made a promise to Abu. "One day we'll be rich, live in a palace, and never have any problems at all," he vowed.

Princess Jasmine would have laughed if she'd heard Aladdin say people in palaces have no troubles. She had to marry a prince by her next birthday, three days away.

Jasmine shared her worries with Rajah, her pet tiger. She was interrupted by the Sultan. "You've got to stop rejecting every prince who comes to call," he warned her.

"If I do marry, Father, I want it to be for love," replied Jasmine. "I've never done a thing on my own. I've never had real friends. I've never even been outside the palace walls!"

"But, Jasmine, you're a princess," protested her father.

"Maybe I don't want to be a princess," Jasmine frowned.

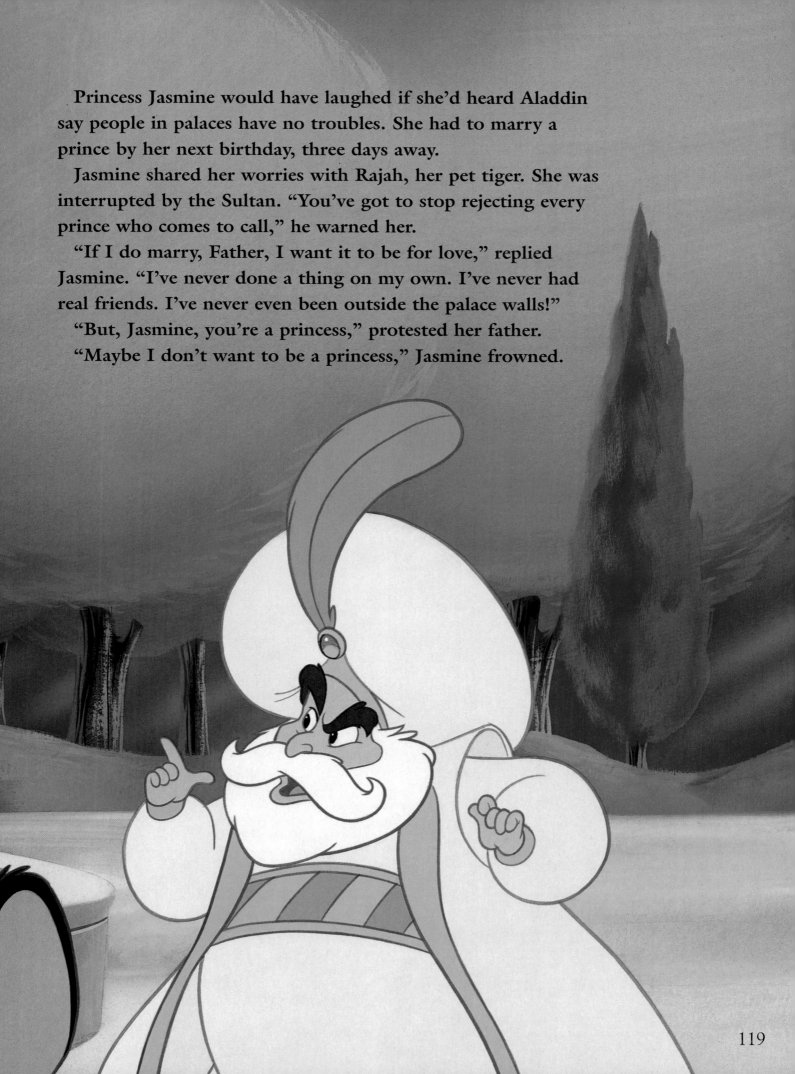

119

The Sultan was in a sorry state. "I'm at my wit's end," he told his trusted adviser, Jafar.

"I have a solution," Jafar said coyly. "But it requires your Mystique Blue Diamond."

"My ring?" protested the Sultan. "But...but..."

Jafar hypnotized the Sultan, hissing, "You will give me the diamond."

"Whatever you need," the Sultan answered.

Grabbing the ring, Jafar stepped into a hidden passageway that led to his sorcerer's laboratory.

"Soon I will be Sultan, not that half-witted twit!" Jafar told Iago. "Just as soon as I find the one who can get us the lamp—the diamond in the rough!"

While Jafar plotted and planned, Jasmine acted on her dream. Disguising herself as a commoner, she made her way out of the palace. Only Rajah was there to see her escape.

"I'm sorry," she told him. "I can't stay here and have my life lived for me. I'll miss you." And she was gone.

Suddenly Jasmine found herself in a world she'd only dreamed about. Everywhere were crowds of people, new smells, new sights, new sounds. There were snake charmers, fire eaters, and hungry children.

Taking an apple from a stand, Jasmine handed it to one little boy. "Here you go," the Princess smiled.

"You better be able to pay for that!" thundered the shopkeeper.

"Pay?" stammered Jasmine. "But I don't have any money."

"Thief!" screamed the vendor as he lunged at her.

Suddenly a young man stepped out of the crowd and grabbed the vendor's arm. "Thank you, kind sir. I'm glad you found her," he said.

"You know this girl?" asked the shopkeeper.

"Sadly, yes. She is my crazy sister. Come along, sis," Aladdin said as he led Jasmine away. "Time to go see the doctor."

Meanwhile, Jafar's secret laboratory was crackling with lightning bolts and wicked plots. Using the Mystique Blue Diamond, Jafar commanded, "Show me the one who can enter the cave." Aladdin was revealed.

"There he is," cooed Jafar, "my diamond in the rough. I'll just have the guards extend him an invitation to the palace."

When Aladdin had first spied Jasmine in the marketplace, a peculiar thing had happened. His pulse began racing. His heart started pounding. He suddenly felt he had to know this girl and everything about her.

"Where are you from?" asked Aladdin as he sat with Jasmine on his rooftop.

"What does it matter?" she replied. "I ran away and I am not going back."

As Jasmine and Aladdin sat and talked, the day grew dreamy, quiet, soft, romantic...at least until the palace guards pushed their way up the stairs. "Here you are!" they bellowed.

"They're after me!" cried Jasmine and Aladdin together.

"They're after you?" Jasmine and Aladdin said to each other.

Then there was no time to talk. Throwing Jasmine aside, the guards rushed at Aladdin. "It's the dungeon for you, boy!" they said.

Throwing back her scarf, Jasmine declared, "Unhand him!"

"Sorry, Princess," said the shocked captain of the guards. "My orders come from Jafar."

Once back in the palace, the Princess confronted Jafar. "The guards took a boy from the market on your orders."

"The boy was a criminal," Jafar replied. "He was sentenced to die."

"What was his crime?" asked Jasmine.

"Kidnapping the Princess," said Jafar.

"He didn't kidnap me. I ran away," the Princess retorted.

"Oh, dear," mocked Jafar. "Had I but known! Too bad the boy's sentence has already been carried out."

But Aladdin hadn't been sentenced to death—just to a cold, dark dungeon cell.

"A princess!" an astonished Aladdin told Abu. "What would she want with a street rat? She deserves a prince. I'm a fool."

"You're only a fool if you give up, boy." It was Jafar, disguised as an old prisoner. He told Aladdin, "Come with me, boy. There is a cave—a cave of wonders, filled with treasures enough to impress even your princess."

Leading Aladdin and Abu out of the dungeon, the disguised Jafar brought them to the Cave of Wonders. "Bring me the lamp!" cried Jafar as the cave rose from the sand.

Carefully, Aladdin approached the monstrous tiger head as it roared, "Who disturbs my slumber?"

"It is I," said Aladdin.

"Proceed," thundered the voice of the cave.

Aladdin and Abu followed the steep steps down, down, down, until they found a huge chamber filled with mounds of treasure!

"Just a handful of this would make me richer than the Sultan!" exclaimed Aladdin.

But he knew better than to take it, for the tiger head had warned, "Touch nothing but the lamp."

Oddly, though, as Aladdin and Abu explored the cave, something kept trying to get their attention. Abu saw it first—a richly embroidered carpet playing hide and seek with him from behind a pile of gold coins.

"A magic carpet!" cried Aladdin when he spied it. "Come on out. We're not going to hurt you. Maybe you can help us. We're trying to find the lamp."

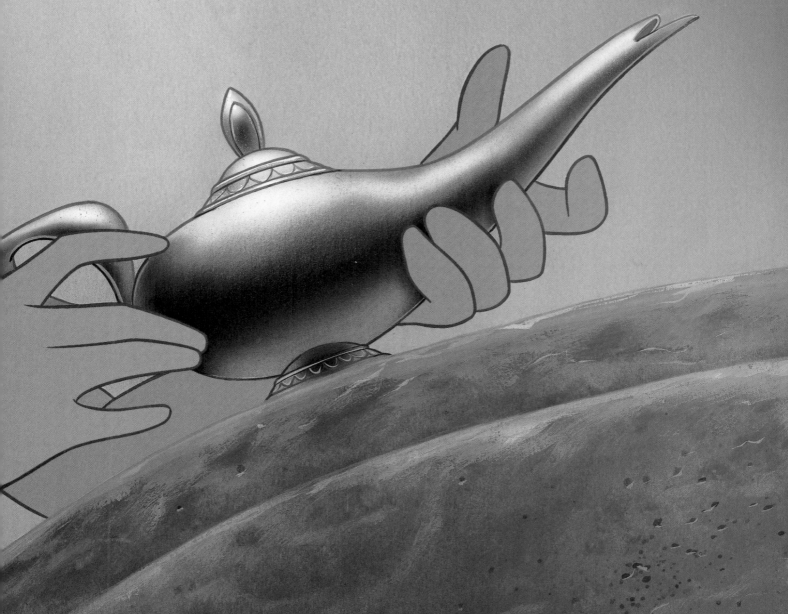

The carpet led Aladdin deeper and deeper into the cave. At last they came to a great underwater lake. In its center was a huge altar of rocks. And at its top, glowing in a radiant light, sat the lamp. One by one, Aladdin scaled
the rocks until he stood before it.

"This is it, Abu?" asked Aladdin as he picked up an ordinary-looking lamp. "This is what we came for?"

But Abu wasn't paying attention. His eyes were riveted on the hands of a statue holding a huge gem. As he lunged for it, the carpet tried to hold him back.

Aladdin shouted, "Abu! No!" But it was too late.

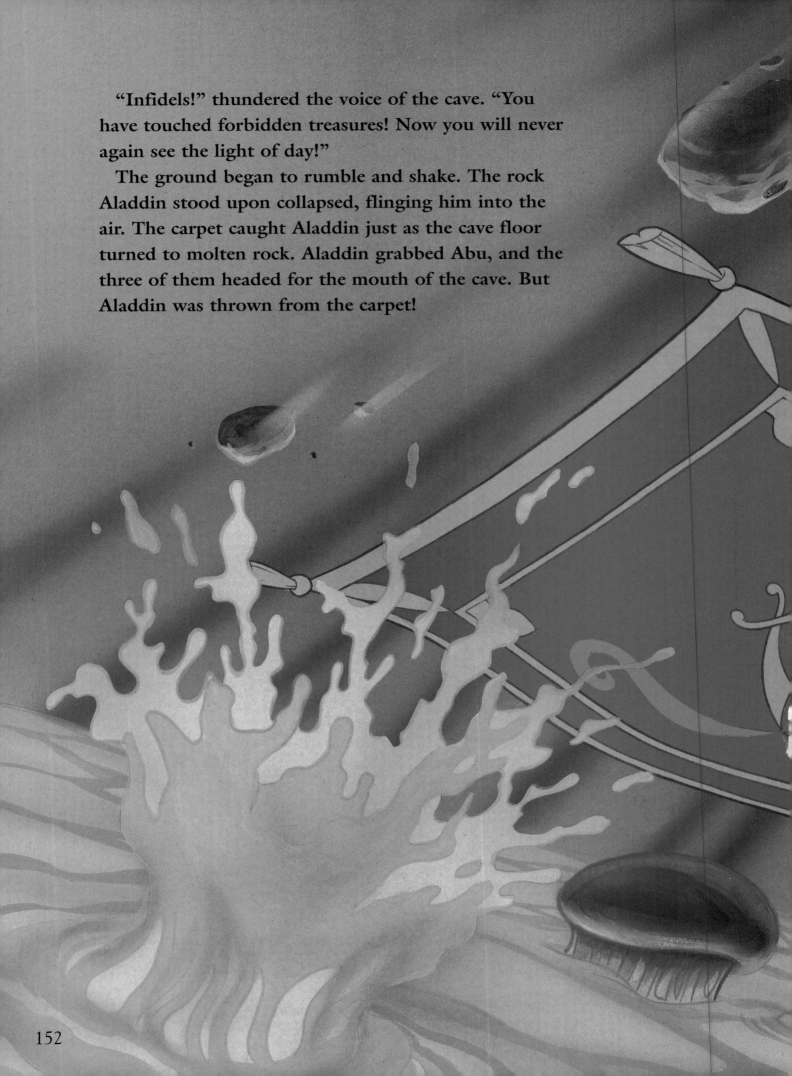

"Infidels!" thundered the voice of the cave. "You have touched forbidden treasures! Now you will never again see the light of day!"

The ground began to rumble and shake. The rock Aladdin stood upon collapsed, flinging him into the air. The carpet caught Aladdin just as the cave floor turned to molten rock. Aladdin grabbed Abu, and the three of them headed for the mouth of the cave. But Aladdin was thrown from the carpet!

Struggling to hold onto the side of the crumbling cave, Aladdin begged Jafar for help.

"First give me the lamp!" said Jafar as he seized it from Aladdin. Then he drew a dagger from his cloak.

"What are you doing?" asked Aladdin in shock.

"Giving you your eternal reward!" crowed Jafar as he struck at Aladdin. But Abu grabbed Jafar's hand and bit down hard. Jafar pulled away in pain as Aladdin and Abu tumbled back into the cave.

"That two-faced son a jackal!" exclaimed Aladdin as he sat trapped inside the cave. "Whoever he was, he's long gone with that lamp."

Abu just smiled. Then he pulled the lamp from inside his vest and offered it to Aladdin.

"Why, you hairy little thief!" laughed Aladdin.

"It looks like a beat-up, worthless piece of junk," Aladdin said, turning the lamp over and over. "Wait—I think there's something written here. It's hard to make out." Aladdin rubbed the lamp.

Sparks flew, smoke swirled, and suddenly a genie appeared!

"Does it ever feel good to be out of there!" the Genie shouted. "Ten thousand years will give you such a crick in the neck!"

Then the Genie told Aladdin, "You get three wishes, and ix-nay on the wishing for more wishes."

"Some all-powerful genie," said Aladdin, winking at Abu. "You probably can't even get us out of this cave."

"Are you looking at me? Did you rub my lamp? Did you wake me up? Sit down and keep your hands inside the carpet! We're out of here!" The Genie took up Aladdin's challenge and they swooped out of the cave.

Meanwhile, at the palace, an angry Jasmine told her father about Aladdin. Even this great wrong didn't make the Sultan doubt Jafar. But Jasmine did.

"Some good will come from my being forced to marry," she told him. "When I am Queen, I will have the power to get rid of you."

"Not if you become her husband," whispered Iago in Jafar's ear. "Then you become the Sultan!"

Aladdin had a very different idea about the man the Princess should marry. "Can you make me a prince?" he asked the Genie. It was done with the wave of a hand.

"Now for mode of transportation," said the Genie, eyeing Abu. "What better way to make your entrance into Agrabah than riding your very own elephant?" Presto! Abu was transformed. "Talk about trunk space!" laughed the Genie.

Gliding up to the Sultan's throne on his magic carpet, Aladdin bowed. "I have journeyed from afar to seek your daughter's hand," said the Prince.

"Prince Ali Ababwa, I'm delighted to meet you," said the Sultan.

But Jasmine was not so easily impressed. "How dare you!" she stormed at her father and Aladdin. "Standing around deciding my future. I am not some prize to be won."

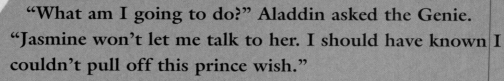

"What am I going to do?" Aladdin asked the Genie. "Jasmine won't let me talk to her. I should have known I couldn't pull off this prince wish."

"Tell her the truth!" advised the Genie.

"No way! If Jasmine found out I was some crummy street rat, she'd laugh at me," Aladdin sighed.

That night, Aladdin did his best to impress Jasmine. But all she said was "leave me alone."

Saddened, Aladdin told her, "You're right. You aren't some prize to be won. You should be free to make your own choice."

That did it. The next thing Aladdin knew, he and Jasmine were soaring through a dazzling sky on the magic carpet.

By the time Aladdin returned Jasmine to the palace, she knew the man she wanted to marry. "Goodnight, my prince," she whispered.

Floating back to Earth, Aladdin told himself, "For the first time in my life, things are starting to go right."

That's when Jafar's men jumped him! "You've worn out your welcome, Prince Abooboo," threatened Jafar. Then, tying him up and gagging him, they threw Aladdin into the sea!

Aladdin dropped like a stone! But as he sank into unconsciousness, the sand rubbed the lamp.

"It never fails," complained the Genie. "Get in the bath, there's a rub on the lamp." Then he saw Aladdin. "Al? Kid! Snap out of it. I can't help you unless you make a wish!"

But Aladdin was too far gone to reply. Shaking Aladdin's head up and down, the Genie said, "I'll take that for a yes." And he carried Aladdin to the surface.

Believing he'd rid the world of Prince Ali, Jafar hypnotized the Sultan into telling Jasmine, "I've chosen a husband for you. You will wed Jafar."

"Never!" she cried. "I choose Prince Ali."

"Prince Ali left," said Jafar.

"Check your crystal ball again, Jafar," said Aladdin as he entered the Sultan's throne room. "Tell them how you tried to kill me, Jafar."

"He's obviously lying," claimed Jafar, as he pulled away from the guards. Then, with a whoosh, he disappeared!

Safe in his secret laboratory, Jafar sent Iago to steal the magic lamp from Aladdin's room. Once the lamp was in his possession, the power of the Genie was Jafar's to control.

"I am your master now!" thundered Jafar. "I wish to rule on high as Sultan."

And the Genie was forced to obey.

Instantly, the peaceful, sunny kingdom turned dark as doom. Jafar was transformed into the Sultan. And as the people of Agrabah watched in horror, the Genie reached down and plucked the palace up, up, up into the air.

Jumping on his magic carpet, Aladdin tried to defend the real Sultan and Jasmine. "Genie! No!" he cried.

"Sorry, kid," said the Genie. "I've got a new master now."

Sending sparks flying from his magic staff, Jafar started a whirlwind that pushed Aladdin and Abu into a tower of the palace and shot them to the very ends of the earth.

Chattering with the cold, Aladdin cradled the freezing Abu in his arms. "This is all my fault," said Aladdin as he began to walk through the high snowdrifts. "Somehow I've got to go back and set things right."

Meanwhile, back in Agrabah, Jafar was doing his best to destroy the Sultan and Jasmine. It looked hopeless until Jasmine spotted Aladdin, who had made his way back on the magic carpet. Determined to distract Jafar, Jasmine pulled his beard and whispered in his ear, "I never realized how incredibly handsome you are."

Aladdin saw his chance and hurled himself at Jafar. Lifting his staff, Jafar cried out, "How many times do I have to kill you, boy?" Then the wicked sorcerer surrounded himself with a wall of flames, and the lamp with a circle of swords.

"Afraid to fight me yourself, you cowardly snake?" taunted Aladdin.

"A snake, am I?" Jafar replied. Then, changing himself into a gigantic snake, he turned on Aladdin.

Striking out with his sword, Aladdin slashed at Jafar. Howling with pain, Jafar summoned up all of his strength and knocked the sword out of Aladdin's hand.

"You thought you could defeat the most powerful being on Earth?" hissed Jafar. "Without the Genie, you're nothing!"

We'll see about that, thought Aladdin. Then he called to Jafar, "The Genie has more power than you'll ever have! He gave you your power, and he can take it away. You're still second best."

"I make my third wish," Jafar commanded the Genie. "I wish to be an all-powerful genie!" And it was done.

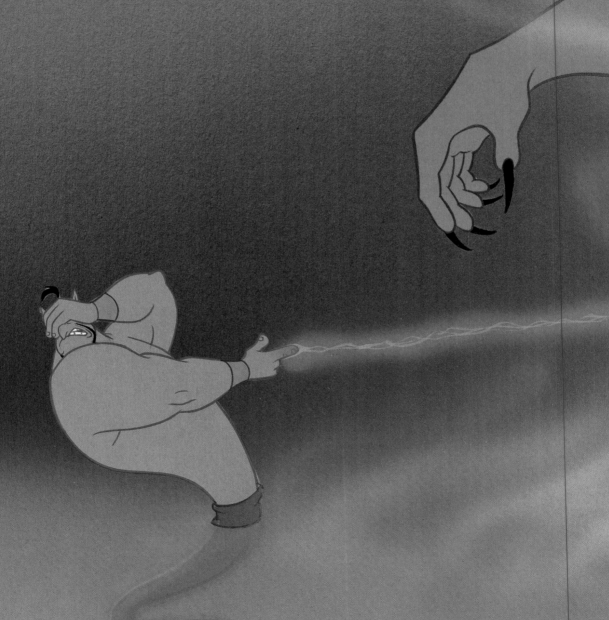

"The universe is mine to command!" cackled Jafar.

"Not so fast," said Aladdin. "Aren't you forgetting something? You wanted to be a genie—you got it. And everything that goes with it!" He picked up the magic lamp and imprisoned Jafar inside.

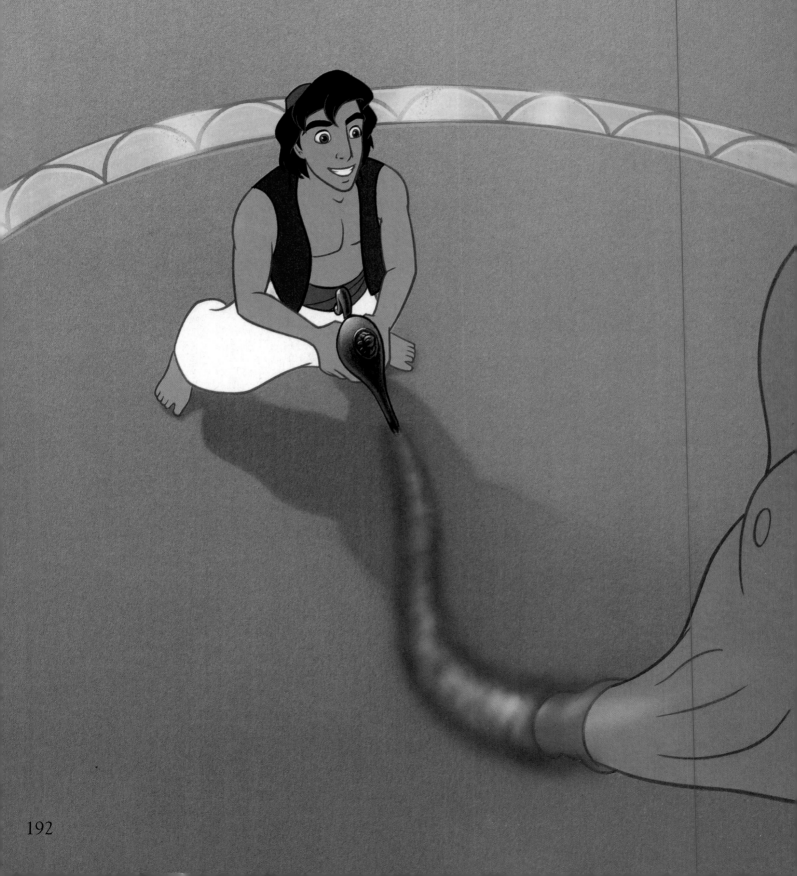

The ending was happy for everyone...except Aladdin. "Guess this is good-bye," he told the Princess.

"That stupid law," said Jasmine.

"From this day forth, you shall marry the man you choose," said the Sultan.

"I choose you...Aladdin," said Jasmine. And suddenly, for a street rat whose heart shone like a diamond, it felt like a whole new world.

Adapted by Victoria Saxon

THE APE MOTHER

A baby's cry drew Kala away from her ape family. The cry was coming from a strange house, high up in a tree's branches.

Inside the house, Kala found the baby. When she held him, he stopped crying and began to laugh with her.

Suddenly, Sabor, a ferocious leopard, sprang at them. Kala risked her own life to save the baby.

Kala brought the baby to her family.

"You cannot keep it," said Kerchak, the apes' leader. "It's not our kind."

"Sabor killed his family," Kala explained.

Reluctantly, Kerchak agreed to let her raise the child. Kala named the baby Tarzan.

As he grew, Tarzan tried to fit in with his ape family. "I'd love to hang out with you," his friend Terk told Tarzan. "But the guys, they need a little convincing."

"What do I gotta do?" asked Tarzan gamely.

"Well you gotta . . . uh . . . go get an elephant hair," Terk said.

To Terk's surprise, Tarzan leaped from the cliff and swam toward the huge creatures!

When Tarzan grabbed an elephant's tail, all the elephants began to trumpet and scramble about in fear. They started to stampede!

The charging elephants rushed through the apes' feeding area. Kerchak leaped to rescue a baby ape just in time.

At the water's edge, Terk ran to Tarzan. "Come on, buddy!" she cried. "Don't die on me." As Tantor, a baby elephant, looked on worriedly, Tarzan revived.

Then Kerchak arrived. Tarzan took all the blame for the stampede. "Tarzan will never fit into this family," Kerchak shouted at Kala.

That evening, Tarzan knelt at the edge of a pool and looked at his reflection. Kala approached.

"Why am I so different?" Tarzan asked, placing his hands against Kala's. Kala gently put her son's head to her heart. "Inside we're the same," she said. "Kerchak just can't see that."

Tarzan smiled. "I'll make him see it," he said. "I'll be the best ape ever!"

As Tarzan grew, he learned to swim like the hippos, swing from vines like the monkeys, and surf along mossy tree limbs.

And when Sabor attacked the apes, Tarzan swung to the rescue with his spear and saved Kerchak's life! Tarzan lifted the slain leopard and let out a victory yell.

Respectfully, Tarzan laid the slain leopard at Kerchak's feet.

Then, a gunshot rang out! Kerchak hurried the apes deeper into the jungle, but Tarzan was curious. He searched for the creature that had made the strange noise.

STRANGERS IN THE JUNGLE

From a treetop, Tarzan studied the first humans he had ever seen.

"Mr. Clayton, your gunshots may be scaring off the gorillas," said Jane to her guide.

"Look! A gorilla nest!" exclaimed Professor Porter, Jane's father. Porter and Clayton pressed on, looking for more nests.

As Jane sketched a baby baboon, the small creature grabbed the picture from her. Jane snatched it back and a group of angry baboons began to chase her.

She turned and ran from the mob when . . . whoosh! Tarzan swooped her into the air.

Safe at last, Tarzan looked at Jane intently. Then he placed his hand against hers. She was like him!

Tarzan pointed to himself. "Tarzan," he said.

"Jane," she replied, pointing to herself.

"Jane," Tarzan repeated, smiling.

Meanwhile, Terk, Tantor, and their friends had found the humans' camp. Terk touched the typewriter. Another ape dropped a plate. The new sounds were fun!

"I feel something happenin' here!" cried Terk. She was rollicking to an all-out jam session when Tarzan and Jane arrived.

When Tarzan led Jane into the camp, she was surprised to see how he greeted Terk. "He's one of them!" Jane gasped. Then an angry Kerchak arrived and Tarzan had to leave with his gorilla family.

Kerchak ordered the gorillas to stay away from the strangers.
Tarzan objected, "They mean us no harm!"
Then Tarzan turned to his mother. "Why didn't you tell me there
were others like me?" he asked.
But Kala did not answer him.

The next day, Tarzan returned to the humans' camp.
Tarzan fascinated Professor Porter.
"He moves like an ape but looks like a man!" Porter exclaimed.

Jane and her father taught Tarzan about the human world. Tarzan, who could imitate almost any animal in the jungle, was now quickly learning English.

Tarzan showed Jane his world, too.

One day when Tarzan arrived at the camp, he realized that Jane was leaving. The boat had arrived to take her back to England.

Clayton told Tarzan, "If only she could have spent time with the gorillas . . ."

"Then Jane would stay?" Tarzan asked. Clayton nodded, smiling slyly. "I'll do it," said Tarzan.

So Terk and Tantor distracted Kerchak while Tarzan led Jane and the others to meet his ape family.

TWO WORLDS MEET

Jane and Porter loved the apes at first sight.

Tarzan spoke to the apes. "Oo-oo-ee-eh-ou."

Jane repeated his sounds and the baby apes cheered. "What did I say?" she asked.

"That Jane stays with Tarzan," he replied with a grin.

Then Kerchak returned—just as Clayton began arguing with a gorilla.
Enraged, Kerchak leaped to protect the gorilla from Clayton.
"Run!" Tarzan shouted. He tackled Kerchak while the humans escaped.

"You betrayed us all!" Kerchak told Tarzan.

Kala saw that Tarzan was torn between his love for his ape family and his need to be with the humans. Though she risked losing him forever, she led him to the tree house where she had found him.

Tarzan dressed in his father's clothes. Embracing Kala, he said, "No matter where I go, you will always be my mother."

Tarzan ran to the beach to catch up with Jane. Boarding the ship, Tarzan cast a sad glance back at his jungle home.

"Tarzan!" Jane cried in warning. But it was too late. Clayton and his evil companions ambushed Tarzan.

Clayton revealed his terrible plan. He wanted to capture the gorillas and sell them! Tarzan yelled in anguish—he had betrayed his family.

Tarzan's cry echoed deep in the jungle. Hearing it, Tantor charged to the rescue with Terk in tow!

With a crash, Tantor broke through the ship's deck, freeing Tarzan and the others. Tarzan swung quickly to the ape's nesting area, but Clayton had already captured Kerchak.

As Tarzan freed him, Kerchak said, "You came back."

"No, I came home," Tarzan replied.

Jane and Porter arrived with Terk and Tantor. Jane swung down on a vine and knocked one of Clayton's thugs aside.

"I'm going to have you out of this in a second," she told Kala.

As Jane freed Kala, a shot rang out. Clayton had shot Tarzan in the arm! Clayton fired again, but this time Kerchak leaped between Tarzan and the bullet.

Wounded, the large ape fell to the ground. Now it was up to Tarzan to protect his family. Tarzan led Clayton up into the tall jungle trees.

Lunging at Tarzan, Clayton fell to his death.

Tarzan ran back to Kerchak. "Forgive me," Tarzan said.

With his final words, Kerchak told Tarzan, "Take care of our family, my son."

The next day Tarzan and Jane said good-bye.

Rowing toward the ship, Porter said, "Jane, dear, I can't help feeling that you should stay. You love him."

Jane knew her father was right. She jumped out of the boat—and so did Porter!

"Oo-oo-ee-eh-ou," Jane said. She and her father were staying.
They were welcomed to their new home by all the apes . . . and by
Tarzan, who knew at last where he belonged.

There once was a house in London where a family named Darling lived. There were Mr. and Mrs. Darling and their three children, Wendy, John, and Michael. Watching over the children was Nana, the nursemaid, who also happened to be a dog. It was to this home that a most interesting visitor came on one magical starry night. His name was Peter Pan.

Peter Pan chose this house for one very special reason: There were people there who believed in him. Not Mr. Darling. He only thought about business and the importance of being on time and dressing properly. But Mrs. Darling was still young enough at heart to believe that Peter Pan was the spirit of youth.

Then there were John and Michael. They knew how to fight off pirates, whoop like Indians, and march like soldiers. To them Peter Pan was certainly real, and they made him the hero of all their games.

But the expert on Peter Pan was Wendy. She knew everything there was to know about him.

On this particular night, after Michael and John had drawn a pirate map on their father's shirt front, Mr. Darling angrily declared, "Children need to grow up." Then, turning to Wendy, he added, "This is your last night in the nursery, young lady."

"And there will be no more dogs for nursemaids in this house," Mr. Darling concluded as he marched Nana outside, where he tied her up for the night.

That's how it came to be that when Mr. and Mrs. Darling went out to a party later that night, Wendy, Michael, and John were left all alone, asleep in their room.

A certain boy and his pixie, Tinker Bell, took advantage of the moment and slipped in through the nursery window.

The Darlings' nursery was a familiar place to Peter. He liked to sit in the shadows and listen to Wendy's stories. The hero of these stories was always Peter Pan, of course. But on his last visit, Peter had gotten separated from his shadow. Tonight he had come to get it back.

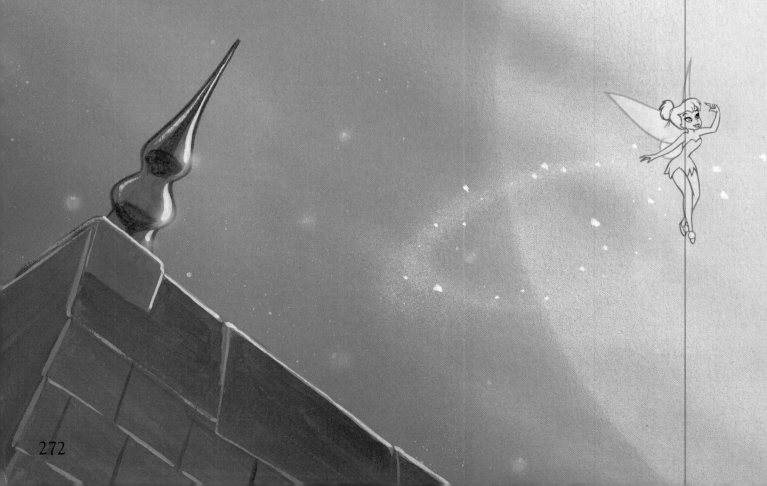

"Well done, Tink, you've found it!" Peter crowed when Tinker Bell discovered his shadow. But the shadow was in no hurry to be following Peter again. The moment he opened the drawer where it was hiding, the shadow took off, flitting and skittering around the room! Peter charged after it, making such a racket that Wendy woke up!

"Peter Pan! I knew you'd come!" Wendy cried. Then she ran to get her sewing basket. "I saved your shadow for you. It needs sewing on. That's the proper way to do it.

"Oh, Peter, I'm so glad you came back tonight, because it's my last night in the nursery," she added.

"But that means no more stories!" cried Peter. "I won't have it! Come on! We're going to Never Land. You'll never grow up there!"

"John! Michael! Wake up...Peter's taking us to Never Land!" cried Wendy. "But Peter, how do we get there?"

"Fly, of course. It's easy. All you have to do is think a wonderful thought. And," said Peter, shaking Tinker Bell, "add a little bit of pixie dust."

"We can fly!" shouted Wendy, John, and Michael as they followed Peter and Tink out the nursery window. They soared over the rooftops of London and past the great clock tower of Big Ben. Peter laughed with glee as he pointed up into the sky.

"There it is, Wendy—Never Land...second star to the right and straight on till morning."

From high up in the sky, they finally spotted the land of their dreams.

"Look, John," cried Wendy, "Mermaid Lagoon!"

"And the Indian Camp!" yelled John.

"There's the pirate ship and its crew," added Michael, all twinkly with excitement. "It's just as you told us, Wendy!"

"Oh, Peter! It's just as I've always dreamed it would be," Wendy smiled.

The captain of the pirate ship was a nasty fellow named Hook. He had only one dream in life—to destroy Peter Pan. "Blast that Peter Pan!" said Hook as he studied a map of Never Land. "If I could only find his hideout, I'd trap him."

Captain Hook got his name because he had a hook where a hand should be. And who was to blame for that? Why, Peter Pan, of course. Hook had another enemy, too—the crocodile. He was terrified of the creature. "He's been following me around for years, licking his chops," said Hook.

"And he'd have had you by now, Cap'n, if he hadn't swallowed that alarm clock. Now when he's about, he warns you with his tick-tock, tick-tock..." said Smee.

"Peter Pan, ahoy!" cried the lookout. Instantly Captain Hook forgot about the crocodile. "Swoggle me eyes," he cried, looking through his telescope. "It is Pan!" Ordering his men to load the cannon, Hook fired away!

"Quick, Tink!" shouted Peter as the cannonballs flew by. "Take Wendy and the boys to the island! I'll stay here and draw the pirates' fire!"

Tinker Bell took off at once for Peter's hideaway. But she purposely flew too fast, leaving the others far behind.

"Tinker Bell! Wait for us! We can't keep up with you!" yelled Wendy and the boys.

But Tink didn't want to wait. Peter Pan had hardly looked at Tinker Bell since Wendy had come along. Tink didn't like it one bit, and now she had a plan!

Tinker Bell zoomed ahead, flying into an opening in a tree where the Lost Boys and Peter lived. Jingling in her pixie language, she told the boys Peter had sent her with a message that there was a terrible "Wendy-bird" headed their way. Peter's orders were to shoot it down!

The Lost Boys hurried out from their hiding place.

"I see it!" yelled Skunk as he and the others placed stones in their slingshots.

"Ready...aim...fire!" shouted the boys. Suddenly rocks were flying everywhere, hitting Wendy and sending her tumbling from the sky!

Luckily, Peter Pan arrived just in time to catch Wendy. "Peter...you saved my life," said Wendy, throwing her arms around him.

"I bring you a mother to tell you stories," Peter angrily told the Lost Boys, "and you shoot her down!"

"B-b-but Tink said it was a bird," stammered Cubby.

"She said you said to shoot it," added Rabbit.

"Tinker Bell," said Peter, "you might have killed Wendy! I hereby banish you forever!"

"Please," begged Wendy, feeling sorry for poor Tinker Bell, "not forever!"

"For a week, then!" declared Peter.

Taking Wendy by the hand, Peter flew off to show her Mermaid Lagoon. John and Michael wanted to explore Never Land, too, but had no interest in mermaids. They wanted to see Indians.

"John, you be the leader," declared the Lost Boys. Then, lining up behind him, they marched off into the forest.

As they marched along, the Lost Boys and John made a plan. They would be very clever and capture the Indians!

It might have worked, too, except for one thing—the Indians caught them first.

Michael and John were very frightened until the Lost Boys explained how things worked. "When we win, we turn them loose. When they win, they turn us loose."

But this time the Indian Chief wouldn't set the Lost Boys free. He thought that they had kidnapped his daughter, Tiger Lily.

"You tell me where you hid Princess Tiger Lily," the Chief said, "or you'll burn at the stake!"

Meanwhile, Peter was showing Wendy the beautiful Mermaid Lagoon when he suddenly spotted Hook and Smee rowing by in a small boat. Tied up in back was Tiger Lily! "It looks like they're headed for Skull Rock," Peter whispered to Wendy. "Let's see what they're up to."

Sure enough, Hook was holding Tiger Lily prisoner in Skull Rock. "Tell me the hiding place of Peter Pan and I shall set you free. Hurry, before the tide comes in!" Hook demanded.

Peter was ready to rescue Tiger Lily. "I'll show the old codfish. Stay here, Wendy, and watch the fun!" Then he drew his dagger and challenged Hook to a fight.

Hook slashed at Peter! Peter jumped away just in time! Then Peter pinned the captain, but Hook broke free and fought Peter to the very edge of a cliff.

"I've got you this time, Pan!" he cried.

Peter backed away from Hook.

Hook followed. Aaaahhhh! He went tumbling off the cliff!

"I'll get you for this, Pan!" he yelled. Then, as he fell toward the water, Hook heard a familiar sound…tick-tock, tick-tock, tick-tock. The crocodile was waiting.

"I say, Hook," grinned Peter Pan, "do you hear something?"

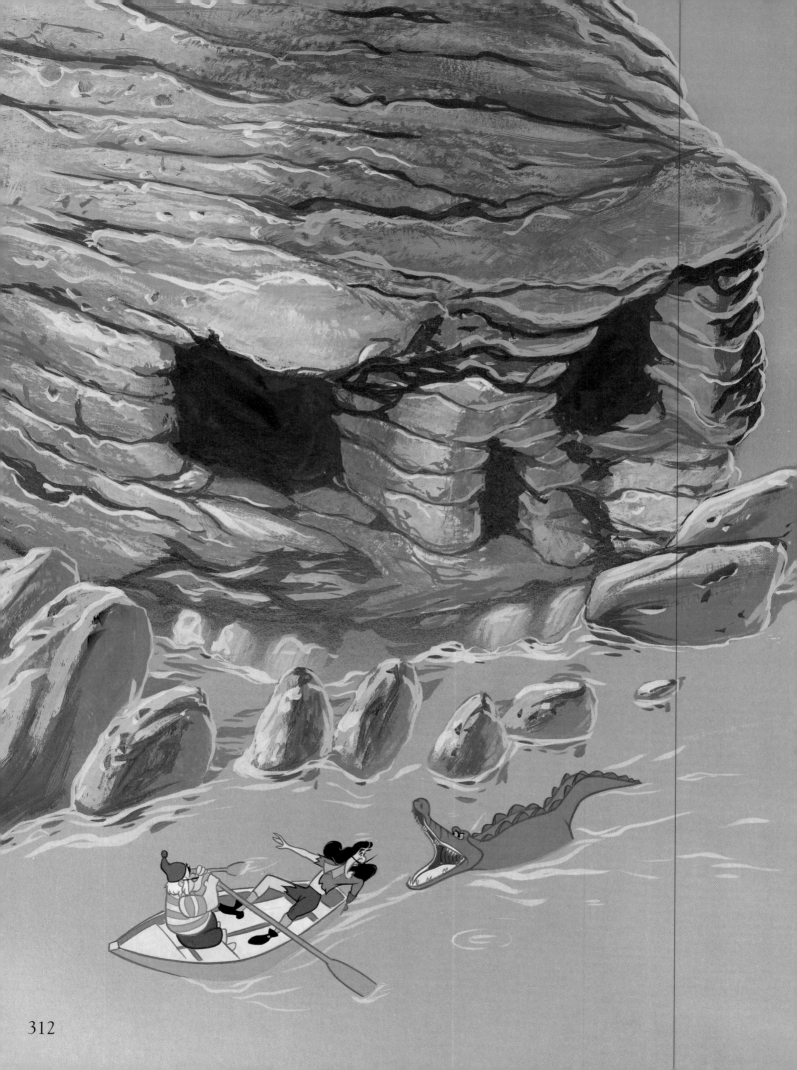

The crocodile swallowed the captain! But the terrified Hook fought
furiously and jumped right back out!

"Smee! Smee!" Hook screamed as he tumbled into the boat. "Row
for the ship! Row for the ship!"

While Smee rowed as fast as he could, Peter swooped down to save
Tiger Lily and fly her back home.

The Indian Chief was so happy to see his daughter again that he freed John, Michael, and the Lost Boys. Then he placed a headdress of beautiful feathers on Peter Pan, proclaiming Peter Pan "Chief Little Flying Eagle."

"Waaawhoop!" yelled Peter.

"Oh, how wonderful!" said Wendy.

"Bravo!" added John.

But there was someone who was not joining in the celebration. Poor Tinker Bell was all alone without Peter or her friends, the Lost Boys. And she wasn't happy at all.

And that's just how Smee found Tinker Bell...all alone, sitting by herself. "Beggin' your pardon, Miss Bell," said Smee, catching Tinker Bell in his knit cap, "but Cap'n Hook would like a word with you."

The Captain wanted a word, all right—several of them. "We sail in the morning," he told Tinker Bell. If she would only tell him where Peter's hideout was, why, he'd take Wendy to sea with him. "With her gone, Peter will soon forget this mad infatuation!"

Sick with jealousy and loneliness, Tinker Bell fell for Hook's evil plan and showed him how to find Peter's hideaway!

At Peter's hideaway, all was cozy and quiet. Wendy, acting as a good mother should, was tucking the boys into bed. As she did, she sang to them about the wonders of a real mother.

By the time Wendy had finished her song, John and Michael were so homesick that they wanted to leave for London at once. Even the Lost Boys wanted to go.

But not Peter. "Go back and grow up!" he said stubbornly. "But I'm warnin' you, once you're grown up, you can never come back!"

But no one was listening to Peter. They had only one thought on their minds: a mother to love them and hold them and sing them to sleep at night. One by one, the boys left Peter's hideaway—only to walk right into the arms of the waiting pirates!

"Now to take care of Master Peter Pan!" chuckled Hook as he lowered a beautifully wrapped package into the hideaway.

Knowing what was in the box, Smee asked, "Wouldn't it be more human-like to slit his throat?"

"Aye," laughed Hook, "but I have given Tinker Bell me word not to lay a finger—or a hook—on Peter Pan. And Captain Hook never breaks a promise!"

Tying his prisoners to the mast of his pirate ship, Hook warned them, "Join us or walk the plank."

"Never," declared Wendy. "Peter Pan will save us."

"My dear," said Hook, "we left a present for Peter, a sort of surprise package. I can see our little friend at this very moment, reading the tender note, 'To Peter, with love, from Wendy.' Could he but see within the package, he would find an ingenious little device set so that when it is six o'clock he will be blasted out of Never Land forever!"

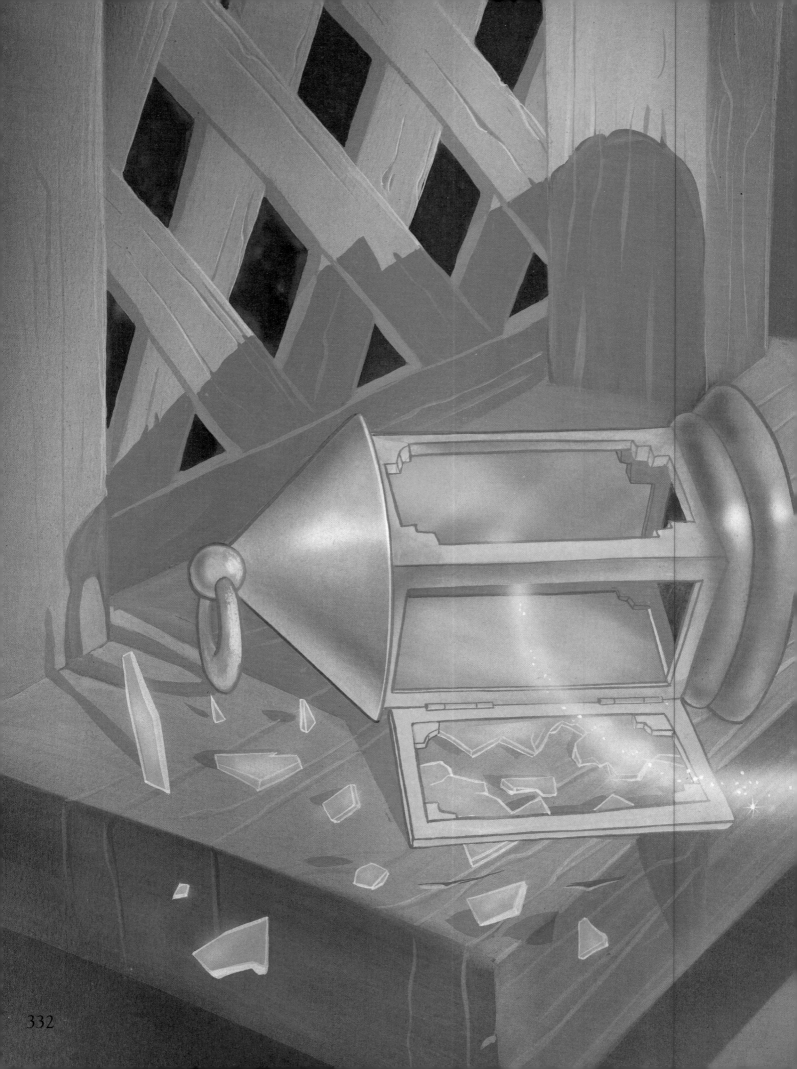

Hearing Hook's evil plan, a desperate Tinker Bell knocked over the lantern where Hook held her prisoner. Crack! went the glass. Tinker Bell was free! Off she flew to try to save Peter.

Back in his hideout, Peter Pan picked up the package and was just untying the bow when Tinker Bell flew in.

"Hi, Tink," said Peter, holding up the box. "Look what Wendy left."

Tinker Bell tried to pull the package away. "Stop that!" yelled Peter. "What's the matter with you?"

There was no time to explain. Tink flew at the box, pushing it as far from Peter as she could. The gift began to smoke. And then...kaboom!

The explosion was so huge, it rocked the pirate ship! Hook removed his hat and bowed. "And so passeth a worthy opponent!"

Smiling, Hook turned to the captive children. "Which will it be? Join me crew or walk the plank!"

Wendy spoke up bravely. "Captain Hook, we will never join your crew."

Hook gave Wendy his most gentlemanly bow. "Ladies first, my dear!" With tears trickling down her cheeks, Wendy walked the plank. One step, then another, closer and closer to the edge, until finally...she jumped!

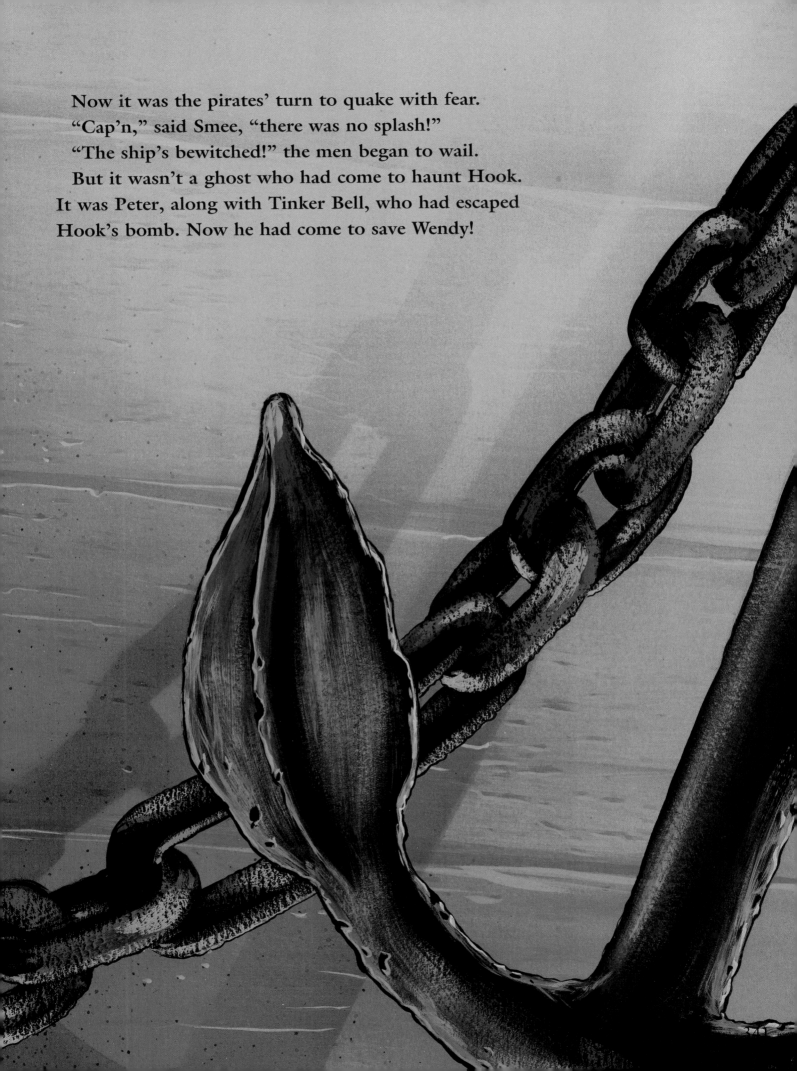

Now it was the pirates' turn to quake with fear.

"Cap'n," said Smee, "there was no splash!"

"The ship's bewitched!" the men began to wail.

But it wasn't a ghost who had come to haunt Hook.
It was Peter, along with Tinker Bell, who had escaped
Hook's bomb. Now he had come to save Wendy!

"This time you've gone too far!" shouted Peter Pan as he flew up onto the rigging. Hook scrambled up after him, then drew his sword.

"Take that!" cried Hook as he lunged at Peter, forcing him off balance. "I'll run you through!"

Peter quickly flew out of Hook's way, cutting this way and that with his dagger.

"You wouldn't dare fight old Hook man to man," taunted the Captain. "You'd fly away like a cowardly sparrow."

"I'll fight you man to man with one hand behind my back!" crowed Peter.

As Wendy, John, Michael, and the Lost Boys fought the pirate crew, Hook took a powerful swing at Peter. But the Captain lost his balance!

Down, down, down fell Captain Hook...to face his worst fear. The crocodile was waiting, and its mouth was wide open!

The last Peter, Wendy, John, Michael, or the Lost Boys heard of the terrible Captain Hook were his calls for help.

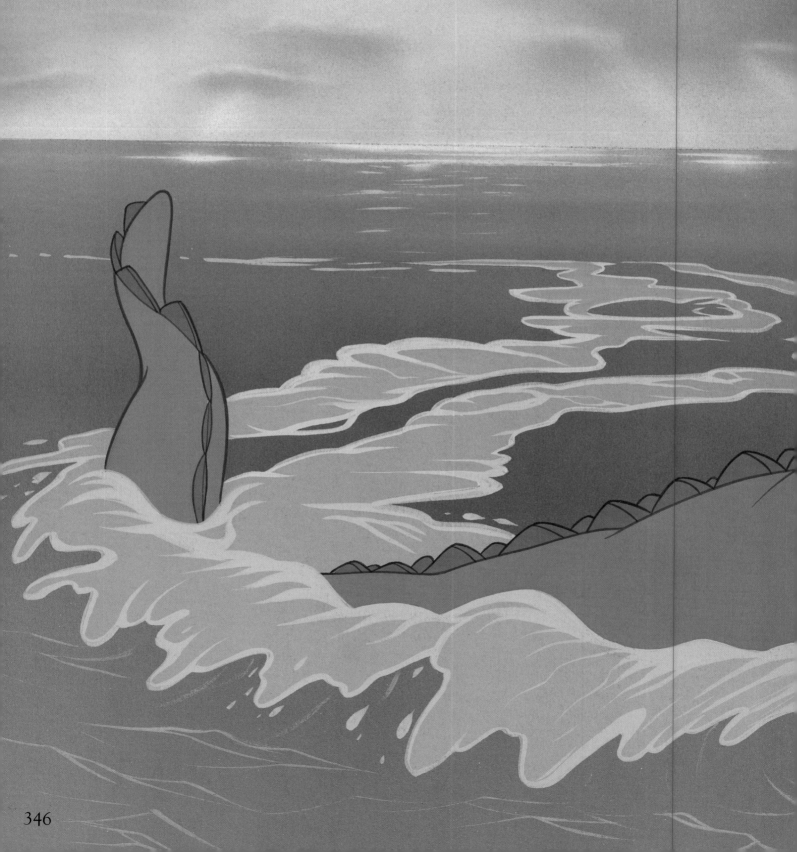

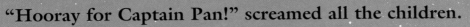

"Hooray for Captain Pan!" screamed all the children.

"All right, ya swabs," said Peter Pan to his brand-new crew, "we're castin' off!"

"But...but...Peter," stammered Wendy, "could you tell me, sir, where we're sailing?"

"To London, madam!" said Peter.

"Michael, John, we're going home!" Wendy smiled.

"Hoist the anchor!" cried Peter to his crew. "Tink, let's have some pixie dust!"

Tinker Bell flew all around the ship, sprinkling her magical dust as she went. Then up, up, up went the ship, and as it rose, it began to glow like gold.

"Wendy," said Mrs. Darling. She was gently shaking her daughter, whom she had found asleep by the window.

"Oh, Mother, we're back!" announced Wendy as she woke.

"Back?" asked Mr. Darling.

"All except the Lost Boys," explained Wendy. "They weren't quite ready to grow up. It was such a wonderful adventure! Tinker Bell and mermaids and Peter Pan. We sailed away in a ship in the sky...."

"Mary," said Mr. Darling, not sharing Wendy's excitement at all, "I'm going to bed."

But as he turned to leave, Mr. Darling paused to look up into the night sky. There, crossing in front of the moon, was a ship made of clouds. "You know," said Mr. Darling, "I have the strangest feeling I've seen that ship before. A long time ago, when I was very young."

And, indeed, he had.